Bella's

BACKYARD BULLIES

SAMANTHA TURNBULL

ILLUSTRATED by
SARAH DAVIS

ALLEN&UNWIN

SYDNEY · MELBOURNE · AUCKLAND · LONDON

First published in 2015

Allen & Unwin
83 Alexander Street
Crows Nest NSW 2065
Australia
Phone: (61 2) 8425 0100
Email: info@allenandunwin.com
Web: www.allenandunwin.com

A Cataloguing-in-Publication entry is available from the
National Library of Australia
www.trove.nla.gov.au

ISBN 978 1 74331 985 7

Cover and text design by Vida & Luke Kelly
Set in 13pt Fairfield LT Std, Light
This book was printed in January 2015 at McPherson's Printing
Group, 76 Nelson St, Maryborough, Victoria 3465, Australia.

www.mcphersonsprinting.com.au

1 3 5 7 9 10 8 6 4 2

For Mum, Dad,
Michael and Charlie

CHAPTER ONE

ANTI-PRINCESS CLUB CHATROOM

MEMBERS ONLINE: 17   **MODERATOR:** Emily Martin

 Emily is online

EMILY: Hi everyone! Bella is right next to me. Grace and Chloe are here too.

WILLA: Is that Bella Singh? The one who designed your amazing treehouse?

EMILY: Sure is – we're in the treehouse now. Bella says hi.

LIBERTY: Hey Bella, can you give us a tour of your treehouse one day? I've heard it's two-storey!

EMILY: Oh, hang on a tick, guys, I just heard a beep and I'm expecting an email from a new member. TTYL.

1

Emily opens her inbox and we all gasp.

Watch your back – OR ELSE.

'Or else, what?' I ask, trying to sound tough.

'What are you looking at, Bella?' Chloe asks.

I point to the unopened email. 'This. It looks like hate mail.'

Grace squints at the monitor. 'It was bound to happen sooner or later. All true celebrities have a crazy stalker or two. That's why they need bodyguards.'

Emily shrugs. 'Exactly 85 days and five hours ago I was a nobody,' she says. 'This wouldn't have happened.'

That's Emily Martin for you: a maths and computer genius who loves to talk numbers. She's also one of my three best friends. The other two, Chloe Karalis and Grace Bennett, join us in a huddle around Emily's laptop.

Until this year, there weren't many people at school who even knew Emily's name, let alone the fact she could code an entire website.

Emily starts tapping numbers into her computer's calculator. 'By my estimation,' she says, 'at least 97 per cent of the 673 students at Newcastle Public School know who I am.'

Emily is not exaggerating. The girl is famous.

She's no movie star. She's not even on one of those lame reality television shows. Who watches those, anyway? If we wanted to see people get makeovers we'd have a front-row seat for live performances at Emily's house – her mum is a beautician with a home salon.

You see, Emily's not well-known in the ordinary sense. She's an internet sensation, and now a president. Not president of Australia – yet. She's the president of … drumroll, please … the Anti-Princess Club.

Emily, Grace, Chloe and I formed the club because we were sick of people trying to turn us into princesses.

The rest of the world, especially our mums and dads, thought girls should behave in a certain manner, look a certain way and be good at certain things. The final straw was when Emily's mum entered her in a spew-worthy beauty pageant.

And that's where the sixth of April comes in. The day of the pageant.

Emily let her mum curl her hair, paint her face and dress her in something so sparkly she looked like a walking string of tinsel. Then, just before she appeared on stage, we helped her change into tracksuit pants and a plain old T-shirt. The real Emily Martin.

She took charge of the microphone and told the crowd why it was wrong to run a contest based on beauty over brains.

Of course, Emily didn't win. But someone in the audience filmed the whole schemozzle and uploaded it to the net. The footage went viral. And that's how Emily became a celebrity.

Within a week, more than a hundred girls had emailed Emily or cornered one of us in the school playground asking to join the Anti-Princess Club. We couldn't fit so many into our headquarters, which is a treehouse in my backyard, so Emily built the Anti-Princess Club website.

We four best friends still hold official club meetings every week, but we also meet with the other club members online. We mostly help them with homework, but sometimes they just want to chat about random stuff.

That's what Emily and I were doing when we found the hate mail.

'I think you need to open it, Emily,' I say. 'Maybe it's just a silly hoax.'

'Okay, here goes,' she says.

Click.

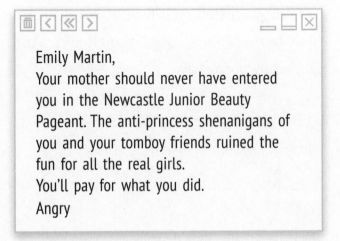

Emily Martin,
Your mother should never have entered you in the Newcastle Junior Beauty Pageant. The anti-princess shenanigans of you and your tomboy friends ruined the fun for all the real girls.
You'll pay for what you did.
Angry

The sender's address is one I don't recognise: catsmum@plutomail.com

'Plutomail is just a generic email service anyone can use,' Emily says. 'But I've no idea who Catsmum is.'

I re-read the email in disbelief.

'What is a real girl, anyway?' Chloe asks. 'We're all real girls, whether we like princesses or not. Who do you think this Angry person is?'

Emily scratches her chin. She does that when she's thinking. 'I don't know. But it looks like Angry is my first official enemy.'

I puff out my chest. 'Then I'm your first official bodyguard.'

Bodyguard Bella. I'll have to break in my new boxing gloves. And nunchucks. And maybe my ninja stars.

CHaPTeR TWO

INGREDIENTS:
250g butter, 120g icing
sugar, 1 egg, 1 tsp vanilla
extract, 300g plain flour,
½ tsp baking powder,
100g chopped almonds,
20 whole cloves, sifted
icing sugar for dusting

'I've finally figured out the perfect recipe for kourabiedes,' Chloe says. 'AKA Andromeda.'

I pull my bum up onto the bench and take a squiz at the list of ingredients. It just looks like a recipe for biscuits to me.

'Koura-what?' I ask. 'And Androm-what?'

Chloe's grandmother appears in the kitchen.

7

'Kourabiedes is Greek shortbread,' she says. 'And Andromeda is a princess from Greek mythology.'

She should know. We call her Yiayia, the Greek word for 'grandmother', because she's from Greece.

'*Yasou*, Bella, hello,' Yiayia adds. 'I thought the club meeting was at your treehouse today?'

'It was,' I say. 'But Mum's letting me sleep here tonight.'

Chloe greets Yiayia with a kiss on the cheek. '*Mana mou* says it's okay too.'

Mana mou means 'my mother'. Chloe's parents are also from Greece, but they moved to Australia before she and her brother Alex were born. They own a restaurant underneath the apartment where they live.

Chloe is an awesome cook, but she doesn't want to work in a kitchen. She wants to be a scientist, so she treats recipes like laboratory experiments – starting with a question, constructing a hypothesis, testing her theories and analysing the results.

'You're correct, Yiayia,' Chloe says. 'But I'm not making Andromeda the princess.'

I thought it was a little strange for an anti-princess to be baking royalty. 'There's another Andromeda?'

Chloe mixes the ingredients in a big silver bowl. 'That's right, Bella. I'm making Andromeda the constellation.'

I spy some star-shaped cookie cutters on the bench.

Yiayia chuckles. '*Paidi mou*,' she says. 'Always coming up with a way to mix science into your chores.'

Chloe kneads the sugary dough. 'Dad asked me to bake some biscuits for the restaurant, so I may as well make them stars. I'll set them up on a tray just as they would appear in the night sky.'

I stick my finger into the bowl for a taste and Chloe playfully taps me on the knuckles with her spoon.

'Astronomy is my favourite type of science,' she says. 'Or maybe it's biology. No, it's chemistry. Although I do like dendrochronology.'

She stops before she lists a branch of science starting with every letter of the alphabet.

'Astronomy is good,' Yiayia says. 'Did you know I saw the first man on the moon? On television, of course.'

That reminds me of the trouble brewing in cyberspace. 'Yiayia, you should read this email Emily was sent.'

Yiayia's reading glasses are dangling on a chain around her neck. She pulls them up to her nose and unfolds the printout I hand her.

She inhales sharply and rests her hand on her heart. '*Tromeros*,' she says. 'Do you know who it's from?'

I shake my head. 'I'm visiting Grace tomorrow morning and we're all meeting at the treehouse in the afternoon to figure out a plan of attack.'

Crack. Chloe bangs a rolling pin on the benchtop. 'You know what I loathe about the myth of Andromeda?' she asks, forcefully pressing the cookie cutters into her dough. 'It's the way Cassiopeia goes around bragging about how beautiful Andromeda is, as if that's all anyone should care about. She's just like Cinderella or Snow White or boring old Sleeping Beauty. Don't princesses have anything to offer other than prettiness?' She pokes a clove into the centre of each star.

Yiayia nods in agreement. 'Yes, it is the bragging about being beautiful that gets Andromeda into trouble.'

I've never read a Greek myth. 'What happens to her?'

Yiayia reaches for an encyclopedia from her collection and heaves the thick book across the table towards me. 'You can read about Andromeda in here, Bella.'

I don't have the heart to tell Yiayia I could

find the story on the internet without lugging such a heavy book home, so I carefully slide it into my backpack.

'Let's just say that after all she's been through, Emily could be the modern-day Andromeda,' Chloe says. 'And it's our job to protect her.'

CHAPTER THREE

Thump, thump. Thump. Thump. A visit to Grace's house can get a little, *thump*, noisy.

Grace lives in a slightly crampy cottage with her mum and dad, plus three brothers, Tom, Oliver and Harry. Luckily she gets a room to herself while the boys have to share.

'Have your parents ever thought about moving one of your brothers in here with you?' I ask. 'Their bedroom must feel like a sardine tin with the three of them in there.'

Grace looks up from the exercise mat. She's bent into what I think is a hamstring stretch.

'You've got to be kidding, Bella,' she says.

'I don't know any girls who share a room with their brothers. I actually wouldn't mind too much, but my dad would never even consider it.'

Grace's dad grew up on a cattle station in the outback with six brothers. Grace reckons his mother was the only woman he'd ever spoken to before he moved away for high school. Even then, he went to an all-boys' college and barely saw a girl until he met Grace's mum. By then he was all grown up.

Thump, thump. Thump. Thump.

Grace rises from the floor and opens her bedroom window. 'Stop kicking that ball against the house!'

'Don't be a sook, princess!' an unfamiliar voice yells back.

I jump to my feet and squeeze my head through the window next to Grace. There are four boys playing with Grace's brothers.

'*What* did you call me?' Grace asks.

Grace's dad hears the fuss and heads

outside. 'Sorry, Grace,' he says. 'I was about to take these guys to the oval for training anyway.'

Mr Bennett is the coach of a junior boys' soccer club. He's still getting used to the fact that his daughter has inherited his athletic talent. His girl-free upbringing meant he'd always considered sport as a boys-only thing.

A smaller boy with a shaved head spits on the ground as the group moves off to the oval down the road.

'Have you ever seen them before?' I ask. 'I can't believe they used the P word on you.'

Grace resumes her floor stretches. 'No idea who they are,' she says. 'I guess they've joined one of Dad's teams. He'll warn them not to mess with me again.'

'How has your dad been?' I ask.

She grabs the edge of the bed and starts a round of tricep dips. 'Better – he's finally agreed to let me swap ballet for athletics training.'

I throw her a high-five from my perch on the bed. 'That's awesome! You can replace those useless ballet jiffies with some high-tech running shoes.'

I hang my head over the bed and look underneath. There it is. A hidden soccer ball.

'When are you going to tell your dad you've taken up soccer too?' I ask.

Grace breaks into star jumps. 'One step at a time, Bella,' she says. 'One step at a time.'

CHAPTER FOUR

Something's out of place, but I can't put my finger on what it is.

I look around the first floor of the treehouse. Cushions on the rug, check. Chocolate jar on the bench, check. Comic books in a stack, check.

Maybe my eyes are playing tricks. I'm constantly moving things around in here. It's the designer in me.

I've still got fifteen minutes before the Anti-Princess Club's meeting, so I open Yiayia's encyclopedia – it's one on Greek mythology. What did Chloe mean when she said Emily could be the modern-day Andromeda?

Andromeda: *the daughter of King Cepheus and Queen Cassiopeia.*

One day, the vain queen boasted about her daughter being the most beautiful in the world. The sea nymphs, who considered themselves quite beautiful, complained to Poseidon, the god of the ocean. Poseidon was angry about the queen's boasting and sent an angry sea monster called Cetus to ravage her kingdom's coastline.

I slam the encyclopedia closed. Now I understand.

Emily's mum, too, thought her daughter was better-looking than everyone else, and that's why she entered her in a pageant. Things didn't go to plan for Cassiopeia, and they sure didn't work out the way Emily's mum hoped either.

The thing is, all the anti-princesses are beautiful. Emily has amazing long red hair and green eyes. Grace is blonde and tall with muscly arms and legs. Chloe has shiny black hair and quirky glasses. As for me, I have brown skin and curls that flow down my back.

When it comes to what looks good, as an artist I consider myself a bit of an expert. And the answer is: there's no right answer.

Some people love watercolour paintings, I like bright comic-book-style posters. We all have our own definition of beautiful. That's why someone was bound to disagree when Queen Cassiopeia claimed her daughter was the prettiest girl on the planet. Duh.

I reopen the book.

Cepheus and Cassiopeia decided to sacrifice Andromeda to Cetus by chaining her to some rocks next to the water.

'Oh, puh-lease!' I yell.

So poor Andromeda was offered up to a sea monster for lunch. And Emily is being threatened by a virtual sea monster – a cyber-bully. That's what Chloe meant.

The hero Perseus saw the princess chained to the rocks while flying past with his winged sandals. He saved Andromeda, then married her.

'Who are you talking to, Bella?' a voice calls from below.

I open the door and see Emily, Chloe and Grace on the grass. 'Come up.'

The anti-princesses climb up and sprawl on the cushions.

'I've just read your Andromeda myth, Chloe,' I tell her. 'And I thought fairytales were bad.

It's just another spew-worthy story about a damsel in distress.'

We call fairytales *unfairy*tales because of the way they make girls seem so helpless.

Chloe rolls her eyes. 'Tell me about it,' she says. 'The princess is rescued by the man in the strange flying shoes. So spew-worthy.'

'It doesn't sound like the type of story that fits our motto,' Grace says, getting up to grab a chocolate.

Then it hits me. Our sign! The Anti-Princess Club motto 'We Don't Need Rescuing' isn't hanging above the entrance to the treehouse. *That's* what's out of place.

'Has anyone seen the sign from above the door?' I ask.

Everyone shakes their heads.

'Never mind.' Maybe I did move it and just can't remember.

Emily clears her throat to get our attention. 'I call this meeting of the Anti-Princess Club to order,' she says. 'I don't think there's any great mystery about what our first matter of business is today.'

Straight to the hate mail it is.

Emily pulls her laptop from its case and flips it open. As the computer fires up we hear voices outside.

I'm standing to go to the window when a soccer ball comes flying through the curtains.

'Look out, Bella!' Grace yells.

The ball bounces off the wall and knocks our chocolate jar off the bench. It shatters on the floor.

'Be careful!' Chloe says. 'There's broken glass everywhere.'

I carefully step through the shards towards the door. The voices outside are getting closer.

'Good shot,' says one.

I peer out and see my brother, Max, with four other boys. 'Who said "good shot"?'

Max looks scared. He knows I'm angry. He points to a bigger boy with hair like a yellow mop.

'You're the boy from Grace's house,' I say. 'Are you the one who called her a princess?'

The boys crack up laughing. All except Max. He knows better than to mess with me, especially since I've started learning how to throw ninja stars.

The other anti-princesses join me in the doorway.

The mop-haired boy sniggers. He looks about eleven, maybe twelve. Not quite old enough for high school.

Emily puts her hands on her hips. 'You think you're funny? You could've hurt someone.'

A middle-sized boy with a blond ponytail puts his hands on his hips. '*You could've hurt someone,*' he mimics in a high-pitched voice.

Emily's face turns red. Like a beetroot. Or a fire engine. Or a beetroot crossed with a fire engine. I have a tube of oil paint in the same

23

shade – it's called Crimson Glory. 'Who ARE you?' she yells.

The boy with the shaved head spits on the ground.

'Give us our ball back!' says the smallest boy, who is wearing a cap.

Grace tiptoes across the glass-littered floor and picks up the boys' soccer ball. 'This one?' She spins it on her right index finger. 'Finders keepers, sorry!'

The mop-haired boy turns to the others. 'Forget about it. We'll get it later.'

They run out of the yard without looking back, leaving Max behind.

'You've got some explaining to do, little brother,' I say. 'Come up here.'

Max drags his feet towards the treehouse.

'Inside,' I say. '*Now.*'

I'm not usually so bossy, but Max needs to learn right from wrong.

Max climbs the ladder. When he sees the glass scattered around the room his eyes widen. 'I'm sorry, Bella,' he says. 'I didn't know they would be so bad.'

Emily puts her arm around Max. 'Who were they?'

I bend down and take one of his hands. 'I know you don't like to be a dobber, but we're not going to let you go until you spill.'

Max sighs. 'They're the Vernons,' he says. 'They're brothers. They just moved here. I was having a kick around with them at the oval – Grace's brothers were there too – and I invited them back here to play some video games.'

Emily unlatches the ceiling flap of the secret storage space I built in the roof of the treehouse. She takes the ball from Grace and throws it inside. 'Well, one thing's for sure, the Vernons, or should I say *vermin*, aren't getting their ball back anytime soon.'

The vermin Vernons and Angry the cyber-bully. Our list of enemies seems to be growing.

CHAPTER FIVE

I don't mean to brag, but my house is big. Really big. I guess you could call it a mansion.

Sometimes, though, I'd rather live in an apartment like Chloe's. It's small but it's never lonely. I'm sleeping over there tonight – and it'll be just me, Chloe and Yiayia at dinner.

'Would you like some tea, Bella?' Yiayia asks.

'Yes, please,' I say.

'Just let me set up my telescope first,' says Chloe. 'I can't wait until it gets dark!'

'Off you go, then,' says Yiayia. 'Don't let tea stand in the way of such excitement.'

Chloe is so lucky to always have Yiayia

around. My mum, who I share a surname with, was born in Delhi and that's where her parents still live. My dad, whose last name is MacKenzie, was born here but his parents live in the Northern Territory. I can count on my fingers how many times I've actually seen any of my grandparents in the flesh.

Yiayia pours us chamomile tea while Chloe sets up her telescope on the balcony. I watch as she assembles the tripod and positions the long tube on top. She takes the cap off the eyepiece and dusts the lens.

'The sky is so clear,' Chloe says. 'Wait until you see what's up there, Bella.'

She comes inside and takes a cup from Yiayia. The three of us start sipping.

'Did you read the myth of Andromeda, Bella?' Yiayia asks.

I pull the encyclopedia from my backpack. 'Yes, Yiayia, thank you for lending this to me. But I didn't like the story much.'

Yiayia smiles and puts the book back on the

shelf. 'I didn't think an anti-princess would approve,' she says. 'But you see now why Cassiopeia should not have cared so much about her daughter's beauty, just like Emily's mama when she put her in that pageant. Is the sea monster still bothering Emily?'

She's talking about the cyberbully. I think 'sea monster' is a good codename.

'We haven't heard any more,' I say. 'But some pesky boys have been giving us a little trouble.'

Chloe's too distracted by the telescope to talk about the vermin. She heads back to the balcony. 'Okay, I think it's dark enough.'

I wrap a blanket around my shoulders and join her. She looks through the telescope and slowly pans across the sky.

'Don't stay too long out there, *paidi mou*,' Yiayia calls. 'You've been out every night this week.'

Chloe lets out an excited 'Yay!' and locks the telescope into place. 'There, that's what I saw last night. Have a look, Bella.'

I switch places with her. The telescope is pointing towards one bright star.

'Wow, Chloe,' I say. 'What is it?'

Chloe is madly jotting down numbers on a piece of paper. They look like coordinates of some sort, but they don't make any sense to me. 'Bella, I think I've discovered a comet,' she says. 'Do you see the tail?'

I look back through the lens and concentrate. I see it, like a fuzzy flying tadpole – the star definitely has a tail.

'Yes, there it is,' I say. 'I think you're right.'

Chloe's positively buzzing now. 'I photographed it last night too, and recorded its position,' she says, setting up her dad's fancy camera on another tripod. 'I didn't want to get my hopes up, because the observatory says it's best to confirm any sighting on a second night. I went online to try to identify it, but couldn't find it anywhere. I can't believe it hasn't been discovered already. This is a dream come true, Bella. We could be making history.'

I feel so proud. Chloe won the science fair last term with her diorama of the solar system, but that doesn't come close to this. Kids like us could be reading about this moment a hundred years from now and dreaming about finding their own comets.

'You could be a star,' I say. 'A star astronomer, that is, not an actual star. You know what I mean.'

We both laugh and take another look into the sky.

I decide our treehouse needs an observation deck. Or maybe a retractable ceiling. Or maybe a planetarium. There's a universe full of possibilities.

CHAPTER SIX

Grace looks like a camel. A single-humped one.

Somehow, she manages to smuggle a soccer ball to school every Monday without her dad noticing how bulbous her backpack is. She's coaching an Anti-Princess Club team. They train once a week during lunch.

Grace shoves her bag into her pigeonhole and takes her seat next to me. 'I've got a great idea for training today, Bella. Can you design a maze I can set up for the team to run through?'

She has barely finished the question before

I'm sketching lines in my art pad. My maze will amaze.

Clip, clop. Clip, clop. It's our teacher, Ms Bayliss, coming down the corridor. She wears sky-high heels that make her teeter like a toddler. I may be a designer, but painful shoes for fashion's sake are something I just don't get.

Clip, clop. Clip, clop. The chatter in the classroom hushes to a murmur as her footsteps become louder. *Clip, clop. Clip, clop.*

I'm madly trying to finish the maze when Grace taps me on the shoulder and moans, 'Oh, great.'

Ms Bayliss is standing in front of the whiteboard with a boy whose blond hair is pulled into a ponytail.

'*Vermin!*' Grace whispers.

It's the second-biggest Vernon brother.

'We have some new students starting at our school today,' Ms Bayliss says. 'And we're lucky enough to have one of them in our class! Please welcome Matt Vernon.'

Grace and I keep still as the rest of the class claps.

Ms Bayliss notices and frowns in our direction. 'Matt and his brothers are quite the soccer players, Grace,' she says. 'So I thought you would have lots in common. Perhaps Matt would like to sit next to you and Bella – you can pull the desks together if you want.'

Matt shakes his head so furiously it's as though Ms Bayliss has asked him to sit next to a live volcano. 'No way.'

He sticks his nose in the air and marches to the back of the room, kicking the leg of our desk on his way past.

'Hey!' Grace yells.

'Er, mind your step, Matt,' Ms Bayliss says. 'Let's get on with today's spelling lesson, shall we?'

I shut my art pad and look at the board. Ms Bayliss starts writing out our weekly spelling list.

Recover
Riddle
Rodent

Grace covers her mouth to hide a giggly snort.

'What is it, Grace?' Ms Bayliss asks.

Grace is struggling to shake her snorts, so I cover for her. 'It's the word "rodent",' I say. 'It just reminds us of a nickname we have for someone.'

Ms Bayliss narrows her eyes suspiciously. 'Sounds like a nasty nickname, girls. That's not like you.' She turns her back and keeps writing.

'The rodents are the horrid ones,' Grace whispers. She writes a note and passes it to me under the desk.

Matt Vernon = Rat Vermin.

CHAPTER SEVEN

I pull some leftover dinner from my lunch box. It's a kati roll, which is a spicy mixture of meat and vegetables wrapped up in flat bread called paratha. Mum doesn't cook much, but when she does it's always something my grandparents used to make her in India.

'What are you up to?' I ask Emily. 'You don't usually bring your laptop to lunch.'

'I just had a quick bit of coding to update on the club website,' Emily says. 'I figured now would be a good time because it's the middle of the school day and no one's online.'

Beep.

'Sounds like you spoke too soon, Emily,' Grace says.

Chloe chuckles as she peers at Emily's screen to see who has just logged in. Then she gulps.

'What is it?' I ask, moving to Emily and Chloe's side of the laptop.

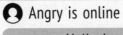

Angry is online

ANGRY: Hello losers.

'How did they get access to the chatroom?' I ask as Emily types back.

EMILY: I see you've heard about the Anti-Princess Club website. Welcome. Care to reveal your real name?

ANGRY: Fat chance.

'Angry had to create an account to get access to our chatroom,' Emily says. 'I'll see what personal details they entered.'

She brings up a page that lists the latest members to join and clicks on the name at the top.

USERNAME:	Angry
REAL NAME:	Angry
EMAIL:	catsmum@plutomail.com
PASSWORD:	cats

'Well, that's no great help,' Emily says. 'I'm going to have to fix this sign-up process to try to stop false names being used.'

She flicks back to the chatroom screen.

EMILY: What is it you want, Angry?
ANGRY: Revenge.

Emily scratches her chin. 'Revenge for what? We haven't done anything to anyone.'

She's right. Our only enemies seem to be the vermin Vernon brothers, but we don't know why they're picking on us, and we don't have any evidence to suggest they're Angry.

I suddenly have an idea. I scan the playground. A couple of girls are skipping nearby, some more are playing handball and a group of boys are sitting on the ground eating their lunch.

'Keep Angry online, Emily,' I say. 'Grace, Chloe, let's do a quick run around to see if we can spy anyone on their computer.'

Grace takes off, and Chloe and I split up to head to other areas of the playground.

I spot the vermin Vernons huddled under a tree near the canteen.

'Hey!' I call out.

Matt looks around, then quickly turns back to the others. They seem to be scrambling over something.

I sprint right up to them as the mop-haired vermin uses his heel to push his backpack underneath a picnic table.

'What do you want?' he asks.

'Got a computer in that bag?'

'So what if I do?' Mop Hair sneers. 'There are hundreds of kids here with computers in their bags.'

Briiiiiing, briiiiiing. Briiiiiing. Briiiiiing.

I stand strong, ignoring the sound signalling the end of lunch.

'That was the beeeelllll, Beeeelllllllaaa,' Mop Hair says. 'You'd better run along to class, Beeeelllllllaaa.'

'Well done,' I say. 'You've learnt my name.'

Emily appears by my side, carrying my backpack. 'Angry logged off a few minutes ago,' she tells me. 'There's no use questioning these guys right now.'

I throw my backpack over my shoulder and head off with her as the vermin Vernons make rude farting noises behind our backs. So original.

'Even if it wasn't completely obvious they were trolling our chatroom, they hate us so much that one of them has got to be Angry,' I say. 'But what have we done to them?'

CHAPTER EIGHT

I'm the only anti-princess on the bus today.

Emily and Chloe live walking distance from school and left for home together. Grace's mum picked her up to take her to athletics practice in the city.

I head for an empty seat next to Jay. His mum is a nurse at the hospital where my parents both work as doctors.

Jay's family comes over to my place for dinner sometimes. He's a pretty good artist too. We painted a mural together on Max's bedroom wall last year: a great white shark eating a killer whale.

'Hi, Jay,' I say. 'What's been happening?'

He shuffles over to make some space. My bum is halfway to the seat when a paper plane hits him in the back of the head.

'What the heck?' Jay asks.

There's laughter from the back of the bus.

It's the vermin Vernons. All four of them sitting together.

'Don't worry about them,' I say. 'They're troublemakers. New in town.'

Another plane glides past my head.

'Awwwww, missed,' a voice says.

Jay cranes his neck around. 'Hey, leave her alone.'

The vermin start a round of 'oohs' and 'aahs'. A couple of other kids join them.

'Are you a *girl* lover?' asks the littlest vermin.

I roll my eyes. I remember boys like this from second grade. They'd run around the swings, yelling 'girl germs, girl germs' as if we carried some sort of infectious disease.

'Grow up, vermin,' I say. 'Oops, I mean Vernons.'

Matt Vernon, AKA Rat Vermin, cracks his knuckles and walks over to our seat. 'What did you call us?' he asks.

'Sit down back there!' our bus driver calls out.

Jay ignores him and stands up to meet Rat Vermin face-to-face. 'I told you to leave her alone.'

Now this is totally unacceptable. Jay knows I'm an anti-princess. I don't need rescuing!

I wedge my arms between Jay's and Rat's chests and push them apart.

'Get over it,' I say. 'It was just a stupid paper plane, and not a very good one at that. Don't you know the difference between a glider and a jet? You should've made a heavier nose and sleek, small wings if you wanted to get any speed out of it. Best stick to playdough, *vermin*.'

The bus comes to a halt and I lose my balance. Rat Vermin falls on top of me and scrambles away as if touching me is the most disgusting thing that's ever happened to him.

Our driver storms up the aisle, huffing and puffing. Beads of sweat fly from his bald head as he waves his arms in the air. 'Your parents will be hearing about this!' he yells. 'I want all your names and phone numbers *now*!'

As I dust myself off and write down my mum's number on the driver's clipboard, Rat Vermin hisses in my ear, 'Watch your back.'

Watch your back. I know those words.

CHAPTER

NINE

It's usually Emily who would call an emergency meeting of the Anti-Princess Club. But today, I've taken it upon myself.

'I'm glad you're all here,' I say. 'This is big.'

Grace, Chloe and Emily are sitting on cushions in the treehouse waiting to find out why I've called them over.

I gaze at the ceiling. I wonder if I could turn our secret storage cupboard into a dome for that planetarium.

Emily senses my distraction. My mind does wander when I'm in design mode. 'Earth to Bella. Shall I call the meeting to order?'

I refocus. 'Yes.'

'I declare this emergency meeting of the Anti-Princess Club open,' Emily says. 'What exactly is the emergency, Bella?'

I pin a printed copy of the hate mail to the corkboard on the wall, grab a yellow texta and highlight the subject.

Watch your back – **OR ELSE**.

'Those words,' I say. 'Matt Vernon, AKA Rat Vermin, said those same words after throwing a paper plane at me on the bus this afternoon.'

Grace and Chloe gasp. I can tell they've come up with a verdict already. Matt Vernon – guilty of cyberbullying.

'So he sent the hate mail,' Chloe says. 'That's my hypothesis. I haven't studied much criminology, but there are loads of theories we could test from sociology, psychology or anthropology.'

I turn to Emily. She is the one targeted by

the cyberbully. 'What do you think, Emily?'

She scratches her chin. 'It could just be a coincidence.'

'You're right, Emily,' Chloe admits. 'Correlation doesn't imply causation.'

Emily takes down the piece of paper and studies it again. 'The email talks about the beauty pageant, but that was in April. And the vermin Vernons are new in town…so how would they know about that?'

Emily is super smart, but she's too humble for her own good. She is oblivious to her celebrity status.

'Aren't you forgetting something?' I ask. 'You didn't have to live here to know about the pageant. The footage was all over the internet.'

Emily nods, but she still doesn't seem certain. 'I just don't know,' she says. 'Something doesn't make sense.'

Grace takes the email and re-reads it. 'Catsmum is the username,' she says. 'If only we knew what that meant.'

Emily racks her brain. 'The mum part suggests it's a female, which steers me away from the vermin,' she says. 'And do we know anyone who has a cat they really love?'

We sit thinking of all the people we know who own cats.

'I bet if I did a survey, there would be more than two hundred cat-owning people that go to our school alone,' Emily says. 'If only we could narrow it down to a female who loves her feline so much that she considers it her baby.'

She opens her laptop. 'Let's set a new mission.'

MISSION SEA MONSTER:

Confirm the identity of the cyberbully.

'All in favour?' Emily asks.

Grace, Chloe and I scream in unison: 'Yes!'

It's time to set some rat traps.

CHAPTER TEN

Chloe has invited all the original anti-princesses, as well as Yiayia, to witness her star-making moment at the observatory.

Grace and I live nearby so I doubled her on my bike. Yiayia drove Emily and Chloe in the restaurant van.

'Professor Jenkins will be with you shortly,' says the receptionist behind the front desk. 'Make yourselves comfortable in the foyer.'

Chloe helps Yiayia to a winged chair while the rest of us sit on a couch shaped like a space shuttle.

'I'm so excited,' Chloe says. 'I can't wait to

have my sighting officially confirmed.' She takes a USB stick from her backpack and waves it like a winning lottery ticket.

'What do you think they'll name the comet?' I ask. 'You know, I was with you at the time, so Bella could be a great name.'

I'm joking. Kind of.

Chloe grins at Yiayia. 'Well, the official name will be a combination of letters and numbers,' she says. 'But I'd like to call the comet Eleni.'

'Oh, *paidi mou*.' Yiayia's voice wobbles.

Yiayia's real name is Eleni. It makes complete sense that Chloe would want to name the comet in her honour. Yiayia's her favourite person in the solar system. Or the galaxy. No, the universe.

A woman in pink-framed glasses arrives in the foyer. She actually looks like how I imagine Chloe will look in about thirty years.

'Hello there, I'm Professor Jenkins, the chief astronomer here. You must be Chloe Karalis.' She extends her hand to Yiayia.

Chloe steps up and takes the professor's hand. 'I'm Chloe,' she says. 'Thank you for seeing me.'

Professor Jenkins stares at Chloe, then eventually smiles. 'Sorry, I didn't expect a child, but, looking back, I was constantly gazing through my telescope at your age. I never discovered a comet, mind you.'

Chloe giggles nervously as Professor Jenkins guides us along a corridor lined with framed photographs of constellations and planets. She waves for us to enter a room with a huge round table and about a dozen empty seats. A computer and projector are in the middle of the table and a white screen hangs on the wall.

'Chloe, I'll see the images before I invite my colleagues in,' Professor Jenkins says. 'Just so I can be sure that what we're looking at is a comet and that I'm not wasting anyone else's time.'

Chloe inserts the USB stick into the computer. An icon named 'Bella's first Christmas' pops onto the screen.

Chloe glares at me. 'That's odd,' she says through clenched teeth. 'I created a folder of photos called "Comet Discovery".'

A queasy feeling takes over my tummy. This makes no sense whatsoever.

Professor Jenkins smiles politely. 'Why don't we open that file and see what's inside? There may have been a mix-up with the labelling.'

Chloe inhales deeply. Her hand shakes as she clicks the mouse.

'Oh no,' I whisper.

The screen is filled with a giant photo of me in a nappy and crown, holding a sparkly sceptre.

'My first Christmas,' I say. 'And my first spew-worthy princess presents.'

Chloe tips her bag upside down and scatters pens and papers across the table. 'There obviously *has* been a mix-up,' she says. 'The right USB stick must still be in your lounge room, Bella, or at the treehouse.'

Professor Jenkins raises an eyebrow. 'The treehouse?'

Chloe ran through her presentation with the anti-princesses at my place yesterday. Somehow, she's picked up the stick with my baby photos instead of her comet pics.

'I'll call home,' I say. 'Mum should be there. She might be able to bring it to us. My house is just a few minutes away.'

Professor Jenkins taps her foot. 'Does anyone have a mobile?'

Yiayia smiles sheepishly. 'I can't use those things. The screens are too tiny for my old eyes.'

The only anti-princess who owns a phone is Emily, but she shakes her head. 'I'm so sorry, guys, it's out of credit.'

The professor glances at her watch. 'You can use the phone at reception, but you will need to be quick. I have another appointment to get to.'

I tear back to the foyer and ask the receptionist to dial my home number. She passes me the receiver.

'Hello?' It's Mum.

'Mum, it's Bella.'

'You are in trouble, young lady. The bus driver just called me…'

'Mum, Mum, please, I need you to have a look for…'

'Bella, you're grounded.'

'But…'

'No buts.'

Beep. Beep. Beep. She's hung up. This is a disaster.

I run back along the corridor and pass Professor Jenkins on the way.

'I'm sorry,' she says, 'I need to go. I'm very busy and don't have time for this nonsense.'

I get to the boardroom and find Chloe sitting at the table with her head in her hands. Yiayia is stroking her hair.

'Don't worry, Chloe,' I say. 'We'll find the right stick, and the professor will meet with us again. You'll see. '

Emily grabs a piece of paper from Chloe's pile and scrawls a note in red pen.

Mission Eleni: Prove Chloe's discovery

CHAPTER

ELEVEN

I hug Chloe, Yiayia and Emily goodbye outside the observatory. No one says a word. Sometimes silence is best when you're upset.

I decide to go with Grace to her house. If I'm grounded I may as well make the most of my last afternoon of freedom.

Grace sits on my handlebars and I double her along the four blocks to her street. We're coming up to her driveway when Grace screams, 'Watch out, Bella!'

I squeeze the brakes and the bike screeeeeeeeches to a halt. My back tyre leaves a long black skid mark on the footpath.

As I catch my breath, it takes me a minute to figure out what's wrong.

Not one, not two, but five soccer balls are rolling across the path. Another one appears. And another.

'Where are they coming from?' I ask.

Grace leaps off the handlebars. 'There!'

We spot a figure as it darts behind a jacaranda tree a few metres away.

Grace sprints to the tree. Three boys jump out from behind a row of bins and start running down the street. Big mistake.

Grace sets off at a phenomenal pace and easily catches up to them. She throws her arms around one of the boy's legs, tackling him to the ground. He tries to wriggle away, but Grace is too strong.

I ride closer and realise who it is that she has squished to the ground. Rat Vermin.

'You could've caused an accident,' I say.

Rat just writhes like a slippery fish trying to escape Grace's clutches.

The other vermin Vernons have come to a stop up ahead.

'Come on, Matt!' Mop Hair calls.

Rat sighs and stops struggling. 'I can't move, Mark!' he calls back. 'She's got me!'

The brothers trudge back towards us, admitting defeat. Grace releases Rat and he jumps up. His knees are grazed.

'You okay?' Grace asks him.

Mop Head Mark pushes his injured brother aside. 'Get the balls and take Michael and Marlow home.' He glares at Grace. 'You think you're a boy or something? You're too rough to be a girl.'

Grace folds her arms. 'What's your problem with us?

Mark ignores the question and points at her backpack. 'You've got my ball in there,' he says. 'I want it back.'

Grace clutches it tightly. 'This is not your ball, it's mine. Yours is still at the treehouse.'

'Don't lie. Why would you have a soccer ball in your bag?' Mark lunges for the backpack and Grace quickly steps aside out of his reach.

'It's mine,' she repeats. 'Leave me alone.'

Mark clenches his jaw. I'm not sure if he cares more about the ball or about Grace out-manoeuvring him.

I climb off my bike and morph into Bodyguard Bella. I stand between Mark and Grace. 'Look, vermin Vernon, Grace coaches a soccer team, okay? Of course she owns a soccer ball.'

Mark cackles nastily, like a cat coughing up a fur ball. 'Yeah, right,' he says. 'Well, if that's true, I guess we'll be playing against you in your dad's tournament.'

Grace holds her hand out for him to shake. 'May the best team win.'

Mark ignores Grace's hand. He gives up on the ball and runs off to his brothers.

Grace turns to me. 'Dad hasn't mentioned any tournament. What have I got myself into?'

I pat her on the back. 'Whatever it is, we can handle it,' I say. 'You'll just need to call some extra training sessions, super coach!'

CHAPTER TWELVE

Our driveway is empty, which means Mum and Dad have left for work. That's a good thing. It's been a wild day and I'm not ready for a scolding about the bus fight.

Our babysitter, Louis, is watching TV with Max. I try to sneak past.

'You're a bit late, Bella,' Louis calls. 'Do you know what time it is?'

'Sorry,' I say. 'I think my watch must be broken.'

Louis's eyes return to the cartoons on the TV. He won't tell my parents. He's cool like that.

I decide to check my emails before I begin

the search for Chloe's USB stick of comet
photos. A new message pops onto my screen.

SUBJECT: Oh no, oh no, oh no!!!

FROM: Chloe

The comet photos aren't on my computer
and Dad has wiped his camera card!
Please, please, please tell me you've
found my USB stick! I can't believe I'd do
something so stupid as not make a back-
up! Aaahhhh!

Another email pings in my inbox.

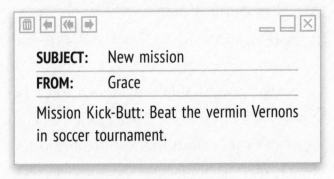

SUBJECT: New mission

FROM: Grace

Mission Kick-Butt: Beat the vermin Vernons
in soccer tournament.

I should've seen Grace's mission coming.

I'm sure the Anti-Princess Club soccer team is up to the challenge, but right now my mind is preoccupied with Mission Eleni.

I run to the lounge room and start rifling through magazines on the coffee table.

'What are you doing?' Louis asks.

'I'm looking for a USB stick, have you seen one?' I ask.

'Haven't seen anything like that here today.'

Max stretches his neck to try to see the TV behind me. 'Me neither,' he says.

'Maybe it's in the treehouse,' I say, running to the kitchen to grab the torch from under the sink.

Outside, my breath makes a fog in front of

my face and a few twigs snap under my boots. The backyard seems kind of eerie tonight. It almost feels as though I'm being watched.

I shine the torch around the yard. 'Hello?'

I think I hear footsteps near the treehouse. I point the light towards the ladder. 'Who's there?'

I keep the light on the ladder and pick up the pace. I don't run. The ground is too uneven and I don't want to trip in the dark.

'Is someone there?' I call again.

I sense movement on the other side of the yard and point the torch at the fence. As my eyes adjust to the darkness, I see a figure just outside of the light cast by my torch.

'You're trespassing!' I yell.

Louis and Max come running out onto the back deck.

'Are you okay, Bella?' Max calls.

I shine the torch towards the back fence just in time to see the top of the trespasser's head as he or she jumps over and runs away.

'There was someone here!' I call back. 'I think they were in the treehouse.'

Max and Louis follow me to the ladder.

'I'm not letting you into the treehouse alone,' Louis says. 'Not now.'

The three of us climb up and I shine the torch around the first floor. The cushions that I stacked earlier are scattered. Half a dozen chocolate wrappers are strewn on the floor. My comics have obviously been rifled through.

'Someone's definitely been here,' Max says. 'I think I heard some strange noises down here last night as well.'

I climb to the second floor and drop to my knees.

'What is it, Bella?' Louis asks.

I point my torch at the wall.

They didn't get to finish. The spray paint is so fresh it's dripping.

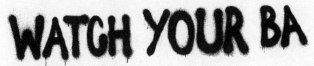

CHAPTER

THIRTEEN

Emily wants to declare war on the Vernons. Her dad is serving overseas in the Army, and he has taught her a thing or two about combat.

'I think one, or all, of the vermin Vernons must be Angry,' I say. 'But how do we prove it?'

Emily paces around the picnic table, scratching her chin. 'There are four of them,' she says. 'And there are four of us.

'Our strategy is simple: isolate and inter-rogate. Without their brothers as reinforce-ments they'll be easier targets.

'Tell your assigned vermin his brothers have confessed if you need to. Don't be afraid to lie

– it's called propaganda.

'As soon as we can rule one brother out, we move to the next one. It will be a simple process of elimination.

'Rest assured, we will find out if the vermin Vernons and Angry are one and the same – and when we do, we'll report them to the police for cyberbullying, trespassing and theft.'

'HUA!' I yell. That's an acronym for 'heard, understood, acknowledged' – Emily's dad says it all the time.

'I'll take Mop Head,' Emily says.

Grace sticks her foot up on the table for a stretch. 'I'll take Rat – I mean, Matt. He won't want to mess with me twice.'

I turn to Chloe. 'Any preference for Michael or Marlow?'

'I guess I'll watch Michael,' Chloe says. 'So you've got Marlow, Bella.'

If only this plan were as simple as putting a piece of cheese in a trap. A giant, human-sized trap. Now *that* would be fun to build.

'We need to follow them home from school today,' Emily says. 'Don't let them out of your sights.'

I groan. 'I'm grounded, Emily. I really should head home straight after the bell.'

The anti-princesses nod politely, but I can tell they're disappointed that I won't be able to track the vermin with them.

'Well…I guess Louis won't dob if I'm just a little late,' I say. 'But I can't stay out after dark.'

CHAPTER FOURTEEN

The vermin Vernons are kicking stones around at the school gate.

Mark stops kicking and stares at us. He isn't used to seeing all four of us here together. He notices we're staring back and turns away as if he doesn't care.

When the bus pulls up, we don't waste time. Chloe runs to Michael, I stand by Marlow, Grace blocks Matt's path and Emily grabs Mark's hand.

'Get out of my way,' Michael says to Chloe. 'I'm sitting with my brothers.'

Chloe won't move. She follows him all the

way to the back of the bus until he's stuck.

'What do you think you're doing?' he asks.

Chloe corners him against the window and braces her foot against the seat in front, blocking his way out.

Grace, Emily and I follow Chloe's lead, each taking a seat next to our assigned vermin.

'You and your friends are lucky you're girls,' Marlow says to me. 'If you were boys we would've punched you by now.'

'Oh, thank you so much for not hurting us poor, weak girls,' I say. 'Personally, I don't hit anyone. Even though I'm highly skilled in ninjutsu.'

So, that's a white lie. I'm still figuring out how to use my nunchucks and ninja stars.

The vermin try to ignore us by staring out the windows, but we're determined to annoy them into reacting.

I start to put the pressure on Marlow. 'You use computers much, Marlow?'

He fiddles with his sneakers.

'Come on, you must have an email address,' I say. 'What is it? I'd love to email you sometime.'

Marlow stares straight ahead. He won't make eye contact.

'You know, I'm not much of a computer guru, but my friend Emily is,' Chloe says to Michael. 'I'm more of a scientist.'

Michael's left eye twitches. Something Chloe said has caught his interest.

'What about you, Michael?' she asks. 'What are you good at? Sending emails?'

'Science,' he blurts out. 'I like science too.'

Chloe is stumped. She didn't expect to have anything in common with the vermin. How could someone so despicable share her passion?

'Why are you so nasty?' she manages to ask.

Michael twiddles his thumbs. 'Well…'

Mark leans across Emily to get Michael's attention. 'Don't say anything,' he tells his little brother. 'She's trying to trick you.'

The bus comes to a stop and Mark grabs his backpack. 'Let's get off, boys,' he says. 'It's a stop early, but it stinks a bit in here.'

The anti-princesses get up too. 'We're coming with you,' Emily says. 'Maybe you should try wearing a little deodorant if you don't like the smell.'

Mark guffaws and walks up the aisle with the other vermin. The anti-princesses follow them down the steps and onto the street, where we power-walk two steps behind them. We refuse to get off their ratty tails.

'Come on, vermin,' I say. 'Which one of you was it?'

We follow them all the way to their front lawn and watch them march into their house. We don't want to get arrested for trespassing, so we park our bums by their mailbox.

'We're not going anywhere!' Grace calls out. 'You can't hide forever!'

There's movement inside. Someone pulls apart the window blinds. A woman peers out.

Then the front door opens and the woman steps outside. She shields her eyes from the late-afternoon sun and squints towards us. 'Emily Martin, is that *you*?'

The woman's white-blonde hair and spindly arms are unmistakable. It's the director of the beauty pageant! Her name is Fiona, but Emily nicknamed her Hungry because she's the thinnest adult we've ever seen.

'Are you here to play with my boys?' Hungry asks. 'They just arrived home. How lovely to have some little girls in the house! Let me set up a tea party for you all!'

Her boys?

Emily's eyes are as wide as my circular saw. Chloe gently elbows her.

'Ah, no, thank you,' Emily says. 'We have to go.'

We all take off around the corner in the direction of Grace's house.

'Hungry is the mother of the vermin Vernons!' I yell. 'I smell a rat – or four.'

CHAPTER FIFTEEN

Grace's dad is leaning over the engine of her family's minivan. He wipes a dipstick on his overalls and slides it back into place.

'Hi, Dad,' Grace says. 'The girls and I are just going inside for a while. They won't be staying too long.'

Mr Bennett slams the bonnet closed. He clenches his teeth and mutters something under his breath.

Grace backpedals. 'What's up? Is there something wrong with the minivan?'

Chloe, Emily and I form a little circle and pretend we're having our own conversation to make it less awkward for Grace and her dad. He seems tense.

Mr Bennett beckons Grace closer and tries to speak quietly. 'Grace, I had a call from someone wanting soccer coaching today.'

Grace shrugs. 'So?'

Her dad slaps himself in the forehead. 'It was the mother of a girl,' he says. 'I thought she was calling because they wanted coaching from me, but she was calling because they wanted coaching from you.'

This time it's Grace who slaps herself in the forehead. It must be hereditary. 'Dad,' she whispers. 'I'm sorry. I was going to tell you. I'm coaching an Anti-Princess Club team. It's not a big deal.'

'I'm trying to be more understanding, Grace,' says her dad. 'I let you quit ballet, I let you take up athletics.'

'I know,' Grace says. 'And I'm so grateful.'

'But I've told you how I was brought up,' he says. 'I'm trying not to be so old-fashioned. I'm just not used to girls. Especially girls like you, and Emily, and Chloe, and Bella.'

Grace's lip starts to quiver and I decide to speak up. 'Grace is very good at soccer, Mr Bennett,' I say. 'She's inherited your skills.'

Grace's dad opens the bonnet again and directs his words towards the engine. 'Anyway, it's not so much that you're playing soccer, Grace,' he says. 'It's that you kept it a secret.'

Grace starts to cry. I think she knows she should have given her dad more credit. All these years Grace has felt misunderstood by her dad, but now she's the one who has made the wrong assumption about him.

'I didn't think you'd let me play,' she sobs.

'Of course I would've let you play, Grace,' he says. 'Soccer is my life. I could've taught you a thing or two.'

Grace wipes her eyes and perks up. 'Well,

now that you mention it, those Vernon boys told me you're organising a tournament soon. Can we enter?'

Mr Bennett checks the dipstick again. 'I think you should go to your room, Grace. I'm disappointed in you for lying to me.'

Chloe, Emily and I follow Grace towards her door.

'Not you three,' her dad says. 'Home for you girls.'

It's probably best I make a move anyway. The sky is turning pink and I should be home by now.

CHAPTER SIXTEEN

Red and blue lights twirl in the distance.

The sun has disappeared, but I'm almost home. I'm pushing my luck with Louis, but he'll be cool. I hope.

As I get closer I realise the blue and red beams are coming from somewhere near my house. Is it an ambulance? I start to run. Maybe Max is hurt.

I round the corner and see a police car.

Oh no. Louis must have called the police when I didn't arrive home on time. Maybe he thought I'd been kidnapped. Are my parents on their way back from the hospital?

'It's okay!' I call out. 'I'm here, I'm here!'

Someone points a torchlight directly into my eyes.

Oouuuuccch.

I'm dazzled by the light and tumble onto the gravel. My palms sting.

A police officer is hovering over me. 'You must be Bella. Isn't it a bit late for a ten-year-old to be coming home?'

She grabs my forearm to help me up. I want to say I don't need rescuing, but something tells me not to argue with the police.

Louis and Max appear by the officer's side.

'Bella, you'd better come inside.' Louis's frowning. It's a worried frown, not an angry one.

I feel terribly guilty. 'I'm sorry, Louis, I didn't mean to get home so late.'

The officer pulls a notepad and pen from her jacket pocket. 'I'm Constable Murphy,' she says. 'Your babysitter is right. Let's go inside. I need to take some statements from all of you.'

She can't be serious. Shouldn't she be

leaving now that I'm home? It's a simple case of a kid coming home late. Case closed. Nothing more to see here.

Louis and Max head inside.

'Follow me, please,' Constable Murphy orders.

I bite my tongue. I've heard you can be charged for arguing with the police, so I allow myself to be led into the house.

Max's breathing is short, sharp and shallow. I ruffle his hair and whisper in his ear. 'Don't worry, buddy,' I say. 'This is all a big fuss about nothing.'

'Mum and Dad are on their way home,' he says. 'This is really bad, Bella.'

Talk about overreacting. 'This is not really bad, Max,' I say. 'I'll tell you what it is – it's ridiculous, with a capital R.'

Louis places his hands on my shoulders. 'Bella, we need you to cooperate.'

I wriggle out of his grip. 'Louis, this is crazy! I'm just a bit late. There was no need to call the police and get Mum and Dad home early from work.'

Constable Murphy smiles a little. 'Bella, that's not why I'm here,' she says. 'I've got more important things to worry about than your curfew.'

Louis and Max point towards the back deck. A breeze blows through the open door and the hairs on my arms stand on end.

I slowly walk to the doorway and look across the yard.

I run down the steps. I trip a couple of times but get straight back up, ignoring the grazes on my shins and the prickles in my palms.

'Be careful, Bella!' Louis calls.

I barely hear him. I just need to get to the treehouse.

I slow down near the trunk and run my finger over the ladder. It's covered in slime. Everything is covered in stinky, sticky slime.

Constable Murphy shines her torch on my hand. 'It's egg,' she says. 'They've thrown eggs everywhere, even inside – you've got quite a clean-up ahead.'

I start wiping the ladder with my sleeve.

'Not just yet,' she says. 'I'd like to take some photos as evidence.'

I slump down on the grass, crunching an eggshell under my bum. Louis and Max squat next to me, hugging me from both sides.

'Did you see what happened?' I ask.

They shake their heads.

'No, but we heard it,' Louis says. 'By the time we got out here they were gone.'

Max squeezes me tightly. 'I'm sorry we didn't see them, Bella.'

Constable Murphy makes a few notes in her pad. 'Whoever did this acted quickly,' she says. 'And there must have been more than one person to create so much mess in such a short time.'

Try four people.

'Do you have any idea who would've done this to your treehouse?'

I don't need to think about that answer for long.

'The Vernons,' I say. 'They've been here before. They stole a sign from above the door, spray-painted one of the inside walls, and took my friend's USB stick.'

They're not just pests. They're criminals.

CHAPTER SEVENTEEN

Emily circles the tree. She's up to her eighth lap when she stops and stomps her feet in anger.

'Aaaaahhh!' she yells. 'I know I declared war on the vermin Vernons, but I didn't mean for your backyard to become a real-life battle-ground, Bella.'

I'm sitting on the frosty grass next to Chloe, shivering in my dressing gown. I'm numb. Not just from the cold, but on the inside too.

Emily and Chloe arrived at dawn. Grace is due any moment.

Mum and Dad forgot I was supposed to be grounded when they saw the egged treehouse.

They called each of the anti-princesses' parents to ask if they could visit me first thing this morning.

'Cleaning eggs off a surface isn't as simple as you'd think,' Chloe says. 'Chemistry comes into play here. We'll need to use water that's hot, but not too hot – eggs are protein-based and we don't want to cook them, or they'll just stick to the walls even more.'

I can't help but smile at Chloe's scientific approach to everything.

Emily, on the other hand, isn't amused. 'This is unbelievable,' she says. 'Those boys aren't just vermin, they're...they're monsters. They've got to be the cyberbully too, don't they?'

She counts on her fingers for a moment. 'It took us about fifteen minutes to get from the Vernons' house to Grace's,' she says. 'And we were only at Grace's place for about fifteen minutes, because her dad wouldn't let us in.'

'Then it took me about fifteen minutes to get home from Grace's,' I say. 'I ran.'

'And during that time Max and Louis heard the noise and called the police, who took about ten minutes to get here. So that means the Vernons had a window of less than thirty-five minutes to get to the treehouse and do their damage,' Emily says. 'They sure know how to cause a fair amount of carnage in a short time.'

Grace arrives with her dad.

'Hi, Mr Bennett,' I say. 'Excuse the mess.'

He takes in the damage to the treehouse. 'You really think the Vernon boys did this?' he asks. 'That's a serious allegation. You'll need to prove it.'

'I told you, Dad,' Grace says. 'They've got it in for us. We think they might even be bullying us online. You should kick them out of your soccer club.'

Emily shrieks. 'Bella, Chloe!' she yells. 'Look at what Mr Bennett is wearing!'

Grace looks her dad up and down. 'It's just his soccer jersey,' she says. 'He wears it almost every day.'

The jersey is yellow and maroon with a cat emblazoned on the chest.

'The vermin Vernons play on your dad's team, right?' Emily asks.

Grace nods.

'And his team is called the *Newcastle Cats*?'

I can almost hear the pennies drop as we realise what Emily's getting at.

'Wait there!' Emily yells.

She scrambles up the treehouse ladder and emerges with a soccer ball. It's the one the vermin Vernons kicked through our window. They mustn't have noticed the flap leading to the secret roof space.

'Mr Bennett, do you recognise this ball?' she asks.

He takes it from Emily and runs his fingers over some letters in black marker. 'MV,' he says. 'Yeah, I guess it belongs to one of the Vernons. All their names begin with M, so I can't be sure which one.'

Emily nods, pretending she actually cares

about the ball's rightful owner. 'Mr Bennett, do you have your mobile phone?'

Grace's dad unclips his phone from the back of his belt and holds it out to Emily.

'Oh, it's not for me,' she says. 'Do you have the Vernons' contact details in there? We'd love to let them know we still have their ball here.'

Mr Bennett starts scrolling through his phone's contacts list. 'I've got Mrs Vernon's number here,' he says.

Grace nudges closer to her dad so she can peek at the screen. 'What about an email address, Dad?'

Mr Bennett pushes a button to bring up extra contact details for Mrs Vernon. 'Catsmum at plutomail dot com,' he reads.

Emily, Grace, Chloe and I let out a simultaneous squeal as Mr Bennett covers his ears.

'Do you think Hungry is Angry, or the boys used her email address to fool us?' I ask.

Grace takes the phone from her dad.

'There's one way to find out.'

Ring, ring. Ring, ring.

'Hello?' says a tired-sounding voice.

Grace panics and passes the phone back to her dad. He puts it on speaker so we can hear.

'Uh, good morning, Mrs Vernon,' Mr Bennett stutters. 'It's Coach Bennett.'

'What can I help you with at this hour? The boys are still in bed.'

I mime some typing.

Mr Bennett nods. 'Um, I just wanted to double-check your email address.'

'Oh, I never really use it. Mark set it up for me – something about a cats' mother – you know, because they play for the Cats and I'm their mum.'

Mr Bennett fakes a little laugh.

'I'll wake one of the boys to check what it is exactly. Hang on…'

'Oh, that won't be necessary.'

'I thought you needed it now – calling so early and all?'

'I've been up training for hours, I didn't think about the time, I'm sorry. Anyway, all I really needed to know was if you used the account, because I'm updating my email database. Thank you, Mrs Vernon. Have a good morning.'

Mr Bennett turns off the phone.

'There's our answer,' Grace says. 'Hungry is Catsmum and the vermin set up her account.'

'Well, we've identified the cyberbullies as the vermin Vernons,' Emily says. 'No great surprise, really. *Mission Sea Monster: complete.*'

'But what now?' Chloe asks. 'The mission was to identify them, but now we need to make them pay.'

Mum appears on the back deck with a cup of coffee for Mr Bennett. 'I couldn't help overhearing that these vicious boys are also responsible for the threatening emails you girls have been receiving,' she says. 'I'm going to call the police and have them add that to their report.'

Mr Bennett thanks Mum for the coffee and takes a sip. 'And I'll look at suspending them from the soccer club,' he says. 'They're proving to be quite the delinquents.'

Grace wrinkles her forehead. 'No, don't do that, Dad. I've got a better idea.'

We all look at her expectantly.

'Just sign the Anti-Princess Club team up to your tournament,' she says. 'And we'll make the vermin Vernons pay on the field.'

Mr Bennett smirks behind his coffee cup, but doesn't commit.

We've still got time to work on him.

CHAPTER EIGHTEEN

A strange contraption is sitting in the middle of Ms Bayliss's desk. It's surrounded by a stack of black paper, a bowl of sand, a packet of rice and a tube of glitter.

It's the time of the week when our class does a science experiment. Chloe's favourite day.

'Who knows what this is?' Ms Bayliss asks.

Chloe's hand darts up. 'It's a record player. It's what people used to play music before computers and MP3 players – even before CDs and those cassette tapes. My yiayia has one.'

'Very good, Chloe.' Ms Bayliss slides a large black disc out of a cardboard case and sits it

on the record player. 'And this is a record.'

Scratchy music begins to play, and the class laughs. It sounds like something from an old movie.

'We're going to be using this today,' Ms Bayliss says. 'But not just to play music.' She points to someone in the back row. 'Yes, Michael?'

Michael? There's no Michael in our class. I turn around and see the ponytailed vermin – Michael.

'I think I did this at my old school,' he says. 'Is it an astronomy experiment? The one where we cut the black paper into circles with a hole in the middle, like a record? Then we stick the sand, rice and glitter to the paper? Then we put the pieces onto the record player so they can spin?'

Ms Bayliss is clearly impressed. 'That's right, Michael,' she says. 'And does anyone know the purpose of this experiment?'

Chloe's hand pops up again. As expected.

'Why is *he* here, Ms Bayliss?' she asks.

Ms Bayliss looks taken aback. 'Michael, even though he is in the grade below you, is an advanced science student, Chloe. He'll be joining our class for our weekly experiment. He's a gifted scientist, just like you.'

I expect Chloe to be fuming over this revelation. A vermin Vernon does not deserve special treatment from Ms Bayliss. And it's absurd to compare anyone's science skills to Chloe's. Except for maybe Marie Curie's.

Michael puts up his hand again. 'The purpose of this experiment is to demonstrate how different types of particles become unique rings of the planet Saturn,' he says.

Urgh, what a show-off. 'Are you going to let him get away with this?' I whisper to Chloe.

Chloe's eyes are fixed on Michael. 'I can't help it if he loves science as much as I do.'

Ms Bayliss starts dividing the materials into piles on her desk. 'You need to get into pairs,' she says. 'And I'd like you all to pair up with someone you've never worked with before.'

I groan under my breath. 'Who are you going to pair up with, then?' I ask Chloe.

'You know that saying, "keep your friends close but your enemies closer"?' she asks. 'I'm going to see exactly how much the vermin knows about science.'

Michael hears her and squirms a little, but shuffles across to make space.

'Well, you're a bigger person than me, Chloe Karalis,' I say. 'I don't think I could stand working with an egg-throwing vermin even if we did like the same school subjects.'

Ms Bayliss grins at Chloe and Michael.

'Jolly good,' she says. 'I knew you two would get along.'

CHAPTER NINETEEN

Right foot, left foot, right foot, left foot. Right. Left. Right. Left.

Grace always says the best way to forget your troubles is to sweat them away.

Emily, Chloe and I are taking her advice and joining in today's Anti-Princess Club soccer team training session. We want to be a part of the team that exterminates the vermin Vernons.

We're running around the oval with the other dozen players. None of us are speaking. We're all focused on putting one foot in front of the other. *Right, left, right, left.*

Phweeeeeeeeeet. 'Back this way, team,' Grace says, beckoning with her whistle. 'I've got a special surprise for you.'

The younger girls sprint to Grace, eager to find out what she's got in store.

Phweeeeeeeeeet. 'Anti-princesses, we have a special guest joining us today. Let's hear a round of applause for Coach Bennett!'

Grace's dad waves from the teachers' car park. He's wearing his yellow and maroon soccer jersey and clutching a clipboard.

The anti-princesses clap as he jogs over and kicks a ball straight into the goal on the other side of the field. He keeps jogging to the nets and everyone follows.

'Let's see if you're as good as my daughter tells me you are,' he says. 'I'll be goalkeeper while each of you takes turns shooting.'

We line up single-file and Grace takes first kick. Her dad dives for the ball but misses and it hits the back of the net.

'Score!' shouts one of the younger players.

There are high-fives all round before Chloe takes a kick. She's the first to admit she's not very good at sport, but what she lacks in skill she makes up for with heart.

Mr Bennett catches the ball effortlessly and rolls it back to us. 'Not bad, Chloe,' he says. 'You almost got there.'

One after the other the anti-princesses take turns. Grace's dad catches four attempts and misses nine. I wonder if he's taking it easy on us.

'Your turn, Bella,' he says. 'Show us what you've got.'

I kick the ball as hard as I can and Mr Bennett leaps into the air. He stretches his arms above his head and catches the ball with the tips of his fingers.

He's certainly not taking it easy on me.

'Good try, Bella,' he says. 'Very high. I almost didn't get it.'

The team seems happy with its performance and so does Mr Bennett. 'I'm pleasantly surprised,' he says. 'You must all train hard.'

Grace mouths, '*I told you so*,' and steps in front of her dad to address the team.

Phweeeeeeeeeet. 'Does everyone think it's time to put forward our proposition?'

Everyone squeals 'YES!' at once.

Grace's dad sighs. 'I should've known I wasn't here for a simple training session. Is this about the tournament again?'

It's time to put the pressure on.

'We want to enter, Dad,' Grace says. 'Pleeease?'

The rest of the team echoes Grace. '*Pleeeeeeease?*'

Grace's dad slaps himself in the forehead. He really ought to break that habit. 'There aren't any girls' teams in the tournament,' he says. 'There's no one for you to play. I'm sorry.'

'What do you mean, there's no one for us to play?' Grace asks. 'There are six teams in that tournament.'

'But they're boys,' says Mr Bennett. 'No girls' teams.'

I can feel the tempers of everyone in the team soaring. We're like a pack of angry wolves about to pounce.

'So?' Grace asks.

'So?' Emily asks.

'So?' Chloe asks.

'So?' I ask.

'SO?' everyone asks.

Grace's dad takes three steps back, as if he's been hit by a gigantic gust of wind. 'I... uh, I ...'

We all take three steps forward. Mr Bennett doesn't back away this time, just takes his hat off and shrugs hopelessly. 'I guess there's no rule to say a team of girls can't enter.'

The anti-princesses break into squeals. Everyone is jumping up and down as if they've already won a match. Or the entire tournament. Or the World Cup.

We're glued together in one big huddle.

Except for Grace. Her arms are in a bear hug grip around her dad.

CHAPTER TWENTY

As much as I try to ignore it, I can't.

The backyard is littered with eggshells. The stinky goo is still stuck to the walls. The police called to say they've got the evidence they needed so we're free to start cleaning up. I just can't muster the energy.

Mum joins me on the deck. She hands me a hot chocolate in my favourite mug – I made it myself on a potter's wheel.

We sip and sadly stare at the slime-covered treehouse.

'I know how upsetting this must be, Bella,' she says. 'That treehouse is almost sacred to you. Building it brought us together as a family, and you've had such special moments with your friends in it. It must feel horrible to have had something so special invaded.'

Mum is right. My first mission when the Anti-Princess Club began was to design and build our headquarters. My whole family helped.

'But you know what?' Mum asks. 'There are two ways you can handle this. One is to feel sad and be angry with the boys. That's probably what they want, you know.'

I hadn't thought of that. I'm sitting here moping while the vermin Vernons are probably kicking a ball around without a care in the world. I'm letting them win.

'The other way to handle this is to see it as an opportunity not just to clean up the treehouse but to give it an entire makeover,' Mum continues. 'I bet you have loads of ideas on how to improve upon the old design or decorate it. You haven't really painted the inside. And, eventually, you can actually be grateful for those boys giving you the motivation to renovate.'

She might be pushing it a little there. I can't imagine ever being thankful to the vermin Vernons for vandalising our headquarters.

I look at the treehouse again. My eyes drift to the second storey. We never seem to use that level. We're always hanging out on the first floor.

'Mum, you've given me an idea,' I say. 'I *have* been thinking about turning the secret storage area in the roof into a planetarium.'

Mum laughs. 'I knew you'd have something up your sleeve,' she says. 'A planetarium sounds like a great plan. A little complicated, but I wouldn't expect anything less from you, Bella.'

I run inside to my room, grab a sketchpad and pencil and start drawing a gigantic dome.

There's a knock on the front door and I hear muffled voices.

'Bella,' Mum calls. 'There's someone here to see you.'

Poo. I loathe being interrupted in the middle of a sketching frenzy. This had better be good.

Constable Murphy is at the door. 'Hello, Bella,' she says. 'We've concluded our investigation into the vandalism of your treehouse.'

I wonder what that means. Have they caught the vermin Vernons? Maybe they're in gaol.

'After some questioning, the Vernon brothers admitted to causing the damage,' Constable Murphy says. 'They've also admitted to sending you some threatening messages online. The question for you is, how do we make them pay for it?'

Mum glares at her. 'Won't they be charged? Isn't that what happens to vandals? Not to mention trespassers, and thieves, and cyber-bullies?'

Constable Murphy looks at us sympa-thetically. 'They're just children. We were hoping you'd have some suggestions on how they could make amends.'

I cut her off. I know exactly how I want the

vermin Vernons to pay – beyond the soccer field.

'They have to help the anti-princesses clean up *and* improve our headquarters,' I say. 'And return our stuff.'

'I'll have a chat to their parents,' Constable Murphy says, making a note in her pad. 'I'm sure they'll be agreeable.'

She clicks her pen and slides it back into her jacket.

'Anti-princesses, hey?' she asks. 'I like the sound of that. I think I might be an anti-princess myself.'

CHAPTER TWENTY-ONE

We call the room below Emily's study the 'torture chamber'. It's her mum's at-home beauty salon.

Every now and then we hear a yelp echo through the floorboards. If I were the architect responsible I would have soundproofed the ground floor.

'Someone must be getting some waxing done,' Emily says.

Chloe looks intrigued. I can tell her definition of 'waxing' is the scientific one: the time of the month when the moon's illuminated surface is getting bigger.

'Not *that* type of waxing, Chloe,' Emily says.

'It's when women get hot wax poured over the hair on their bodies. Then my mum rips it off, pulling the hair off with it.'

Chloe shrieks and rubs her hands across her legs. I wince and smooth down the hair on my arms. Grace covers her eyebrows as if they need protecting.

Emily doesn't bat an eyelid. She's used to the sounds of pain that ring through her house.

'I call this meeting of the Anti-Princess Club to order,' she says. 'Why did you want to meet at my place, Bella?'

'Because the vermin Vernons are at the treehouse at this very moment,' I say.

The anti-princesses gasp, stunned.

'They're on cleaning duty,' I continue. 'As ordered by the police.'

Emily grabs her belly and almost falls over laughing. Chloe hoots and Grace jumps in the air cheering.

'And I'd like to propose another mission,' I say. 'I want to make an addition to the treehouse. I want to build a planetarium.'

The anti-princesses nod enthusiastically – but they don't know the catch.

'And the Vernons will be helping,' I add.

Emily drops her laptop in shock. Grace freezes mid hamstring stretch. Chloe spits out a mouthful of water.

'The police officer in charge of the investigation came back last night,' I say. 'She told me the boys admitted to the damage and she asked me how they might pay for it. Cleaning up was one thing, but it wasn't enough.'

Emily screws up her nose. She can think of a million other ways she'd rather get payback. 'Wouldn't you prefer to see them suffer? Like getting them to scoop up dog poo around town? Or clean some toilets…with their toothbrushes?'

Chloe likes this game. 'How about making them walk to school in their undies? Or singing the national anthem in tiaras and tutus?'

Grace throws in her two cents. 'I think we should make them lick the bottoms of their shoes. Or eat a bunch of the fieriest chillies imported from Mexico.'

The anti-princesses are hilarious – that's one of the reasons I love them. But this is serious.

I try to explain my reasoning. 'They want us to feel sad and defeated, but I want to use this as a chance to make an even more amazing treehouse. And what better way to do that than force them to help?'

We hear a door close and an engine start up. The yelping hairless woman has left.

'Emily, can you come downstairs and help me tidy up?' her mum calls out.

Emily picks up her laptop and speedily types:

Mission Makeover: Add planetarium to the treehouse – with help from the vermin Vernons

'All in favour?' she asks.

Everyone slowly raises their hands.

'I guess so,' Chloe says. 'Although I would've loved to see them in tutus, cleaning toilets and licking the bottoms of their shoes.'

CHAPTER TWENTY-TWO

The piece of black paper is rotating so quickly that the sand, rice and glitter are a blur.

I'm not sure what is spinning more: the record player or my head.

Chloe and Michael Vernon are proudly standing beside their project, watching it spin.

Ms Bayliss sticks gold stars on their shirt collars. 'Good work, guys. Can you explain to the other students what we're seeing here?'

Chloe flicks a switch and the paper slows down. 'When the sand, rice and glitter spin, we see a ring – just like the phenomenon of the rings we see around the planet Saturn.'

Michael turns the record player back on. 'So what we're learning is that Saturn's rings aren't solid. They're are made up of gazillions of small particles that orbit around the planet.'

Chloe smiles at Michael and heads back to her place at our desk.

'There's only one strange phenomenon in this class right now, Chloe,' I tell her. 'And that's your new friendship with the vermin Vernon.'

Chloe elbows me. 'We're not *friends*,' she whispers. 'We were just partners for this project.'

Michael stays at the front of the classroom and whispers something to Ms Bayliss.

Ms Bayliss wheels out a projector, pulls down the blinds and turns off the light. Michael plugs the projector into Ms Bayliss's computer and slips a USB stick into the drive.

A bright star appears on the wall.

The smile quickly disappears from Chloe's face. She looks angry. No, outraged.

Ms Bayliss is awestruck. It's as though she's been slapped in the face with a wet trout. 'Oh

my goodness, is that a comet, Michael?'

I should've known. The vermin Vernon not only stole Chloe's USB stick, he's about to take credit for her discovery.

'Not so fast, vermin!' I shout.

Ms Bayliss swiftly turns on her high heels and points at me. 'Bella Singh, how very rude! I don't know what's come over you. To the principal's office, now.'

'But, Ms Bayliss,' I say. 'You need to know the truth.'

She stomps a heel. 'Out!' she yells, pointing at the door. 'Now!'

Michael holds up two fingers in a peace

sign. 'Whoa,' he says. 'Calm down, everyone.'

'Bella didn't do anything wrong, Ms Bayliss,' Chloe says. 'It's Michael, he stole my USB stick. *He's* the one who should be in trouble.'

Ms Bayliss pulls up the blinds and turns on the light. 'What on *earth* is going on?'

Michael giggles. 'Maybe the question should be, what in *space* is going on?'

Rat Vermin is the only one who laughs.

'I admit I stole your photos, Chloe,' Michael says, wiping the smile from his face. 'Matt swapped your USB stick with another one from Bella's living room. We took it when we were in there playing video games with her little brother.'

I cringe as Matt slumps in his chair.

'But we had no idea what was on your stick, Chloe,' Michael continues. 'I thought it would be some boring homework.'

Chloe crosses her arms. She's not buying Michael's story.

'I couldn't believe it when I saw the filename "Comet Discovery" and then the comet,'

Michael says. 'I wanted to make it up to you by showing the whole class what an amazing discovery you've made.'

Ms Bayliss flops into her chair and takes off her heels, looking fed up. 'So, what you're saying is, Chloe discovered this comet. And you stole her photos.'

Michael blushes. This isn't how he imagined things would turn out. 'I'm sorry. We're already in trouble with the police and our parents. Chloe can have all the photos back now.'

Ms Bayliss ejects the stick from her computer and hands it to Chloe. 'We'd better get these to the observatory quick smart, Chloe. And Michael, *you'd* better go to Mrs O'Neill's office.'

Michael hangs his head. 'Sorry again,' he says. 'But I thought the comet was awesome.'

Chloe curls her fingers around the USB stick. 'Stop,' she calls as Michael opens the door. 'Thank you for saying my discovery is awesome. And thank you for returning the photos.'

Wonders of the universe never cease.

CHAPTER TWENTY-THREE

A sea of striped soccer jerseys gathers around Grace's dad to hear the draw for the tournament.

He passes a piece of paper to me and I push it straight to Grace. I figure she, as captain-coach, deserves the honour of announcing the playing order.

Grace glances at the draw, then folds it up. She's not giving anything away just yet.

'Follow me, anti-princesses,' she says. 'We need to go through our game plan.'

We jog after her to the dressing sheds, where we sit in a circle with Grace in the middle.

Emily can't take the suspense. 'How many

games do we play? Do you need me to calculate the odds of us winning? How about a formula for us to get to the final?'

'There's no maths involved, Emily,' Grace says. 'It's a sudden death tournament.'

One of the younger players swallows loudly, her eyes bulging. I can't help but giggle as I realise she has taken 'sudden death' too literally.

'Sudden death means as soon as you lose a match you're knocked out of the tournament,' Grace explains.

The younger player looks relieved, but Chloe, Emily and I are petrified. A sudden death tournament could mean we don't get to play the vermin Vernons. And if we don't get to play the vermin Vernons we don't get to complete our mission.

The corners of Grace's lips curl up. She throws the paper on the floor and pumps her fists like a boxer getting ready to enter the ring.

'Does that mean what I think it means?' Chloe asks.

Grace laughs. 'It helps having a dad who also happens to be one of the tournament organisers,' she says. 'He knew about our mission to beat the vermin Vernons, so he made sure – with some hassling from me – that we'd go head-to-head in round one!'

Everyone leaps to their feet as Grace starts her pep talk. 'Now, let's not lose focus out there. It only takes one moment of brilliance to win a game.' She touches her toes. 'Dad says the vermin Vernons are great attackers, so we need to be strong in defence. Let's keep them away from the goals. If we can keep them scoreless right to the end, we only need one great shot to claim victory.'

Grace points at me and Chloe. 'Bella, you can put your bodyguard skills to work as a defender. Chloe, I know you're not the most confident player, so just do your best to back up Bella in defence.'

Three other players are allocated defensive positions.

'We'll also have four midfielders,' Grace says. 'And one all-important striker to score that crucial goal we need to win.'

She holds her palm out and everyone stacks a hand on top.

'We all know we're just as good as them,' she says. 'But today we're going to be even better. Goooooooooooo Anti-Princess Club!'

'*Goooooooooooo Anti-Princess Club!*' we repeat, throwing our hands into the air.

Everyone runs out of the sheds to the field. The vermin Vernons and the rest of their team are already in position, waiting to kick off.

'About time,' Matt says. 'Now let's get this over with so we can move on to the games with the *real* teams.'

No one takes the Vernons' bait. We're too focused for lame heckling.

Grace surprises us all by pulling on the goalkeeper's gloves.

Emily counts as everyone takes their places. 'Hang on – that only leaves me as striker.'

Grace kicks her the ball. 'That's right. Like I said, winning the game only takes one moment of precision. Scoring is all about angles – we need a mathematician to plant that goal.'

Emily nods nervously and runs to her spot up the front. She passes the ball to Matt so the game can begin.

A few of the vermin and their teammates laugh. They're positioned much differently, with five forwards and just a few defenders.

Phweeeeeeet.

The boys attack.

The anti-princesses band together in defence, just like Grace told us to. We're like a wall protecting our half of the field. Every time a Vernon tries to get past, an anti-princess blocks him.

'Keep it up, girls!' Grace calls from the goal. 'Don't let them through!'

The boys are fast and strong, but they're lacking one key ingredient: teamwork. Everyone is attacking, but they're too keen to score. No one is passing the ball. They're ball-hogs.

'Pass it to me, Mark!' Matt yells.

Mark keeps the ball and tries to dodge our defence, but we're sticking to him like glue. We're like icing on fingers, but we're not about to get licked.

The half-time whistle blows and Grace calls us into a huddle. 'Great work, anti-princesses,' she says. 'We've followed our game plan and kept the score at nil. They're making it easy by not cooperating with one another. But now, we need to think about getting the ball to Emily so she can score for us.'

The second-half whistle blows and we take our positions.

Emily kicks off and chases the ball. She gets it back after it rebounds off Marlow's shin.

Michael sprints towards her and throws out his leg. He trips her. Deliberately.

Phweeeet. The referee holds up a yellow card.

Grace calls out from the goal: 'Don't let them bully you!'

The Vernons are getting frustrated. I intercept a pass from Matt to Mark and dribble the ball forward. But before I get a chance to kick to Emily, Marlow crashes into me, sending me face-first into the mud.

Phweeeet. The referee holds up a red card.

'But sir!' Marlow says. 'I didn't mean it.'

The referee orders Marlow off the field.

My knees are bleeding. I sure have lost a lot of skin lately. I grit my teeth and get up.

Even with Marlow's absence, I'm scared we won't be able to get the ball to Emily.

Suddenly, I hear Grace's dad from the crowd on the sideline. 'What do you think you're doing?' he shouts. 'You're leaving your end open!'

Grace has left the goal exposed and is dribbling the ball upfield. She easily weaves in and out of the spaces between the shocked boys.

Mark and Matt rush towards her, but she delicately chips the ball over their heads.

Then it happens.

Emily traps the pass from Grace as the Vernons' goalie leaves his spot to cut down

her angle. Before he gets the chance, Emily lines up her right boot and kicks the ball. It sails into the air, following a perfectly U-shaped curve (Emily says it's called a parabola) and lands on the grass beneath the crossbar. The ball rolls into the goal.

'We did it!' I scream.

Phweeeeeeeeet. It's the full-time whistle.

Mission Kick Butt: complete.

CHAPTER TWENTY-FOUR

An announcement booms over the school's loudspeakers.

'Everyone, please make your way to the hall for a special assembly.'

Ms Bayliss puts down her whiteboard marker and claps her hands. 'You heard it,' she says. 'Everyone up and to the hall.'

This is weird. The last special assembly I remember was to check our heads for nits. Everyone had to line up and have their scalps examined with fine-tooth combs. They found a couple of the suckers in my hair. I'm still itching just thinking about it.

'What could it be?' Chloe asks me as we follow the crowds from the neighbouring classrooms to the hall. 'Do you think we're in trouble?'

'I hope not,' I say. 'Mum and Dad only just got over the bus fight.'

Everyone arrives at the hall and sits on the floor. Our knees overlap once we all have our legs crossed. This room could really do with a redesign.

The principal, Mrs O'Neill, takes the stage. 'Good morning, everyone.'

'Good moooooooorrrrrrrrrning, Mrs O'Neill.'

'We have a special guest at school today. Please welcome Professor Jenkins, the chief astronomer at the observatory.'

Chloe squeals quietly.

Mrs O'Neill hands over the microphone to the professor.

'Hello, everyone,' says Professor Jenkins, 'I'm here to tell you about a very important discovery that was made recently right here in Newcastle. Could we have the lights off, please?'

A hush sweeps over the hall. I grab Chloe's hand and clench with all my might as the lights dim. Suddenly, a massive photo of Chloe's comet flashes onto the screen onstage.

'Does anyone know what this is?' Professor Jenkins asks.

A hand appears above the crowd in the middle of the hall. It's a vermin. Michael.

'That's a comet,' he says. 'No doubt about it.'

'That's right.' Professor Jenkins shines a laser pointer at the image. 'And we know it's a comet because of this tail.'

The hall lights brighten and Professor Jenkins scans the crowd.

'The most exciting thing about this comet is that the state observatory has confirmed it has never been seen before,' she says. 'And the person who discovered it is a student at this school.'

'Oohs' and 'aahs' fill the hall. Kids start looking around, trying to figure out who the star astronomer could be.

Chloe closes her eyes, savouring the moment.

'Could everyone please put their hands together for Chloe Karalis,' Professor Jenkins says. 'Chloe, come on up.'

Chloe opens her eyes and makes her way through the crowd towards the stage. She's radiating. Like a star.

'Wooooooot, wooooooo!' I yell. 'Go, Chloe!'

Two voices call out from the opposite side of the room.

'Yeah, Chloe!' Emily screams.

'Hooray for Chloe!' Grace shouts.

Professor Jenkins shakes Chloe's hand and gives her a framed certificate. 'I hereby announce the discovery of Chloe's Comet,' she says. 'Well done.'

Applause erupts, but Chloe brings her index finger to her lips, motioning for everyone to shush.

She takes the microphone from a perplexed Professor Jenkins. 'With respect, professor, I would prefer not to have the comet named after me.'

The professor raises one eyebrow. 'Don't you want to be credited for this discovery? Naming a comet after the person who discovered it is standard practice, not to mention a great honour.'

Chloe hands back the certificate. 'I'd like to name the comet after my grandmother, my yiayia,' she says. 'Her name is Eleni.'

Professor Jenkins takes off her glasses and dabs her eyes with a handkerchief from inside her sleeve. 'What a lovely gesture. We'll reprint this certificate right away. Eleni's Comet it is.'

Applause erupts again. Louder this time.

Mission Eleni: complete.

CHAPTER TWENTY-FIVE

A black van pulls up at the front of my house. A man's head pops out the driver's side window.

'I'm looking for the Singh–MacKenzie residence,' he asks. 'This it?'

Emily, Chloe and Grace surround me. 'Maybe,' I say. 'Who's asking?'

The man turns off the engine and steps outside. 'I'm Monte Vernon,' he says. 'I've got my boys here to help you renovate your treehouse.'

Another MV. Don't the vermin realise there are other letters in the alphabet?

The side door of the van slides open and out hop Mark, Matt, Michael and Marlow.

They seriously don't want to be here. Their bottom lips are hanging so far out, I wonder if they'll stretch to the ground.

'Hang on, I forgot something,' Marlow says. He jumps back in the van and emerges with a plank of wood.

'Oh, it's our club sign,' I say. 'Um, thanks.'

The Vernons' dad shuts the van door. 'Do what the girls tell you, boys,' he says. 'Mum will be back to pick you up tonight.'

The vermin stare at the ground.

'Well, this is nice and awkward,' I say. 'Come into the backyard and we'll show you the tree-house. Not that you haven't seen it before.'

The Vernons shuffle through the house to the back deck.

Mum, Dad and Max helped me dismantle the treehouse roof yesterday. There's a pile of bamboo rods and sheets of plastic next to the tree.

'So, here's the deal,' I say. 'We're adding a dome-shaped frame to the second storey. It will be made from bamboo and covered in plastic.'

Marlow makes a 'hmmmph' sound. Something tells me he's impressed, though he's trying to act cool. 'So you want to build a geodesic dome?' he asks. 'Like the top of a planetarium?'

I'm surprised he understands my artistic vision. 'That's right, ver— I mean Marlow.' I unfurl my blueprint and everyone gathers around.

'That's not bad,' Marlow says. 'I mean, it's going to be pretty lightweight because we're making it from bamboo, but it should be okay.'

'I think you'll be surprised by its strength,' I say. 'Once the triangles are all pieced together

the half sphere will be very sturdy. I could've used wood, aluminium or PVC piping, but I would've needed a team of professional builders.'

Marlow rubs his hands together. 'Well, let's get started,' he says. 'We could even decorate it. A mural on the outside would look awesome.'

I hadn't thought of decorating. All I know is that the inside of the dome will be covered in white plastic so we can project images onto it, and the outside will be black.

I'm tempted to take Marlow back to the house and show him my sketchbooks, but I need to explain the plans to the rest of the group.

'We're going to need sixty-five pieces of bamboo,' I say. 'Thirty-five long pieces, and thirty slightly shorter ones.'

'I'll start measuring,' Emily says.

Mark pulls his own tape measure from his back pocket. 'You can mark the measurements we need and I'll saw them into pieces.'

Emily looks sideways at me.

'It's okay,' I tell her. 'They're here to help.

Marlow, you can help me piece the lengths of bamboo together with eyelet screws and cable ties. Grace and Matt, you two lift the frame, piece by piece, up to the second storey. You're the strongest ones here.'

Grace flexes her biceps a little. They're bigger than Matt's.

'Oh, I know you're strong,' he says. 'You tackled me in the street, remember? And you were pretty much the best player on the field in the soccer tournament.'

Grace starts to climb the ladder. 'Well, you weren't too bad in the soccer game yourself. It's just that no one would pass the ball to you at the right moment.'

'Chloe and Michael, you can cut the plastic to size,' I say. 'And stretch it over the frame once it's put together.'

Before I can say 'planetarium', everyone is getting along as if we'd never had an argument.

Michael looks up at the sky. 'I wish I could discover a comet. You must be stoked, Chloe.'

'You can have a go of my telescope one day if you want,' she says. 'You can spot comets during the day too. Oh, of course you know that.'

We work right through lunchtime until Mum appears on the deck with a tray. 'Hey kids, you haven't eaten,' she says. 'Take a break.'

Marlow frowns at the food on the tray.

'They're samosas,' I say. 'Indian fried pastries filled with potatoes, onions, peas and lentils.'

He takes a bite. 'Yum,' he says. 'They're tasty.'

'We all like a lot of the same things, don't we?' I ask. 'Maybe we should be friends.'

Matt grunts. 'We can't,' he says. 'We promise not to wreck any more of your stuff. Or steal any more of your stuff. Or send any emails about stuff. But we can't be friends.'

I look at Marlow for a response. Surely he has changed his tune after getting to know me.

'Is that what you all think?' I ask.

No one answers.

Emily pegs a pea at the treehouse in disgust. 'You vermin are so immature,' she says. 'Don't you know boys and girls can get along just fine? What are you, preschoolers?'

Mark stands up and confronts Emily, eye to eye. 'Save your speech for the video camera, Emily. You're the one who brought this on.'

The other Vernons gather around Mark. They've got their angry faces on again.

The anti-princesses mirror their pose and back up Emily. It's a gang face-off.

'You're the one who ruined our mum's beauty pageant,' Mark says. 'That video made her the laughing-stock of our neighbourhood. That's why we had to move here to your stupid suburb and to your stupid school.'

The email, the vandalism, the general horridness. It's all falling into place.

'Don't you get it?' Mark asks. 'We had to make you pay for what you did to our mum.'

Emily is mortified. She had no idea she had ruined the lives of Fiona 'Hungry' Vernon and her entire family.

'Come on, boys,' Mark says. 'Let's get this

planetarium built and get out of here.'

For the next four hours, we all piece together bamboo triangles without another word.

Marlow and I place the last five pieces of bamboo to meet at a single point in the centre of the dome.

Chloe and Michael drape the sheet of black plastic over the top of the frame and tack the white piece onto the inside.

The planetarium is done by the time the Vernons' black van arrives in the driveway.

'All finished,' I say. 'An actual planetarium in our treehouse.'

Mission Makeover: complete.

But there's no jumping up and down and cheering like usual when we complete a mission.

Mum appears on the back deck with Hungry. 'Wow, that looks fabulous,' Mum says. 'Good job, everyone.'

They walk across the yard to have a closer look. Hungry takes a snap of us all in front of the tree with her phone. We pull fake, cheesy grins.

'I hope my boys pulled through on their end of the deal,' she says. 'Don't worry, they're still in trouble at home.'

For the first time in history, Emily doesn't know what to say. She's still wracked with guilt for uprooting the Vernon family.

'Mrs Vernon, we'd like to apologise,' I say. 'Your sons were just trying to get back at us because of what we did to you. They wouldn't have been so mean if we hadn't ruined your beauty pageant and your life.'

Hungry's shiny white teeth almost blind us as she smiles. 'Oh, don't be so silly, you didn't ruin my life,' she says. 'That video didn't only make Emily famous, it made me famous too.'

The boys shout together: 'What?!'

'We had to move because of them, Mum!' Mark says. 'We had to start a new school and everything.'

Hungry throws her head back and laughs like a kookaburra. 'Oh boys, is that what you think? We moved closer to the city so I could pursue my modelling career. I need to capitalise on the fame from that pageant video.'

The anti-princesses start giggling. I don't know what's funnier – the thought of Hungry modelling or the looks on the Vernons' faces.

The boys mutter their goodbyes and slink away to the van with their celebrity wannabe mum. Just before they're out of earshot we hear Hungry's last words.

'What were you boys thinking, trying to stick up for me like that?' she asks. 'Don't you know I don't need rescuing?'

EPILOGUE

I love climbing up into the new Anti-Princess Club headquarters. I'm so lucky to have a planetarium in my own backyard.

As I look up at the dome, I think how funny it is that the Vernons helped us build this.

Now that the saga with the eggs and the emails has ended, we anti-princesses have actually become really good friends with them. We don't refer to them as vermin anymore – even behind their backs.

Emily and Mark are always battling against each other in online games. Turns out Mark is quite obsessed with computers too – can't code a website, though.

Grace and Matt meet once a week to practise soccer. Grace's new goal is for the Anti-Princess Club soccer team to win an entire tournament – not just one round like they did last time.

Chloe is forever hanging out with Michael on her apartment balcony with their telescopes. He wants to discover a comet just like she did. And Yiayia is super proud to have had a nucleus made up of ice and dust named after her.

Marlow and I decided to leave the outside of the planetarium black. Any other artwork may have interfered with the projection of images onto the inside of the dome. But we're working together on a design for a cubby in the Vernons' backyard. They don't have any trees, so it has to be on the ground. I'm trying to convince him it should be in the shape of an igloo, but he likes the idea of a pyramid.

His mum takes great delight in watching us

work together after all the drama. 'Who would've thunk it?' she always says.

Speaking of Hungry, she eventually did get a foot in the door of the modelling industry. Literally. She's a foot model. Her left foot featured in a hiking boot ad. All thanks to the Anti-Princess Club making her famous.

Looking back, it seems the Vernons' nastiness was all based on one big misunderstanding. It really had nothing to do with us being girls. The boys just wanted to avenge their mum. I guess they thought they were superheroes or something. Yawn.

Now that we're buddies, I hope they don't try to pull any similar stunts to stick up for us.

Whatever lies ahead, there's one thing I'm certain of: we won't need rescuing.